Erica Helmstetter

Sean Murphy

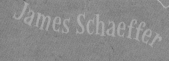

James Schaeffer

Douglas Mayes

Emma Shannon

Trick-or-Treat, SMELL MY FEET!

Lisa Desimini

THE BLUE SKY PRESS · AN IMPRINT OF SCHOLASTIC INC. · NEW YORK

Thank you to my young friends
for all your drawings of smelly socks.

THE BLUE SKY PRESS

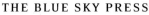

Copyright © 2005 by Lisa Desimini
All rights reserved.

SCHOLASTIC, THE BLUE SKY PRESS, and associated logos are
trademarks and/or registered trademarks of Scholastic Inc.

Library of Congress catalog card number: 2004014823

ISBN 0-439-23323-2

10 9 8 7 6 5 4 3 2 1   05 06 07 08 09

Printed in Singapore 46
First printing, August 2005

FOR MY HUSBAND, MATT

Delia and Ophelia were witch twins
who loved to scare all the children
in the neighborhood.
That's the nature of witches.

On sunny days, the twins
went for a walk with their
fire-powered umbrellas.

On stormy nights,
they made all the lights go out
except theirs.

Today was Halloween, the witches' favorite
day of the year, and they were planning
the spell of all spells.

The main ingredient for their potion was smelly
socks. The twins had been stealing them right
out of their neighbors'
laundry baskets for
the past two weeks.

"Here, kitty, kitty," called Delia.
"Where are you?"
Rufus, who had been turned
white as snow by a spell
gone wrong, was hiding
under the bed.

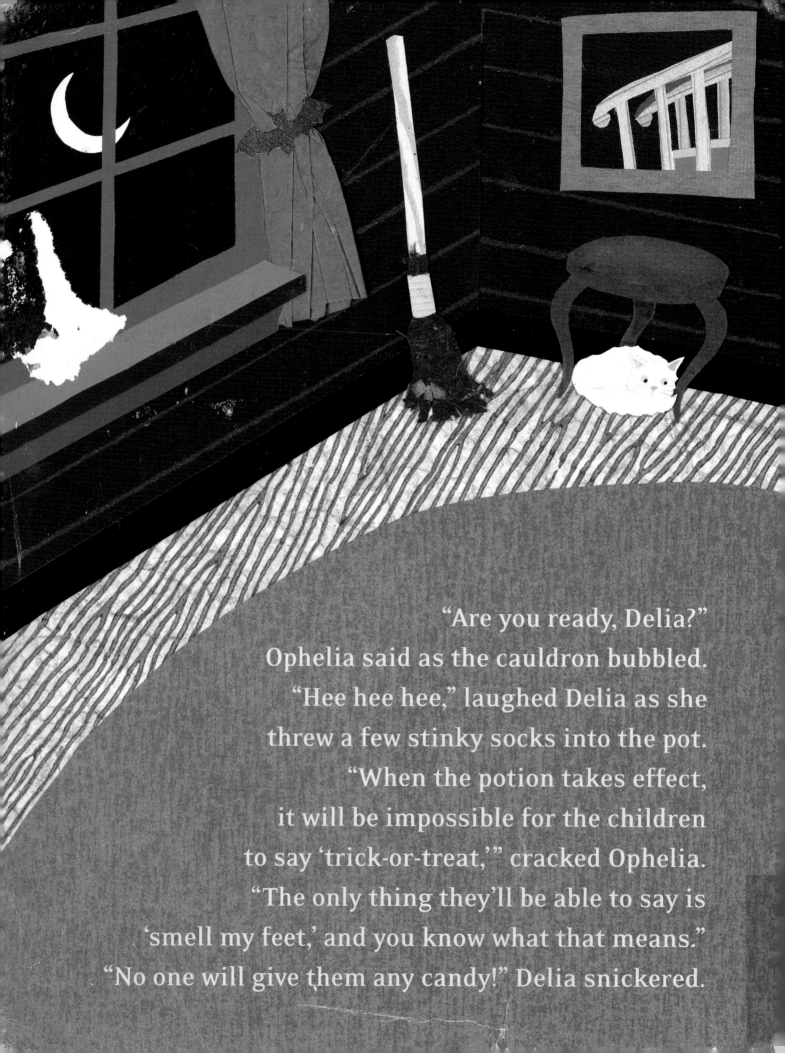

"Are you ready, Delia?"
Ophelia said as the cauldron bubbled.
"Hee hee hee," laughed Delia as she
threw a few stinky socks into the pot.
"When the potion takes effect,
it will be impossible for the children
to say 'trick-or-treat,'" cracked Ophelia.
"The only thing they'll be able to say is
'smell my feet,' and you know what that means."
"No one will give them any candy!" Delia snickered.

"Tee hee hee ha ha hee hee,"
the witch twins laughed and
slapped their knees.

They pulled two chairs up
in front of the window and waited
for the fun to begin.

"Look! Across the street!" Delia
pointed a crooked finger.
"The kids are in their costumes—
ready to get some candy."

"It's time," Ophelia said, grabbing a grubby handful of smelly socks. She threw them into the cauldron and stirred. Now the smoke coming out of the chimney had a slight greenish tint and was spreading across town.

"There's Susie," Ophelia cackled. "She's dressed like a fairy princess."

But when Susie opened her mouth, "smell my feet" is what came out.

"Ha ha haaa," screeched the twins as the door slammed in Susie's face. "No candy for Susie!"

Doors were slammed
on superheroes, pirates,
kitty cats, and ghosts.

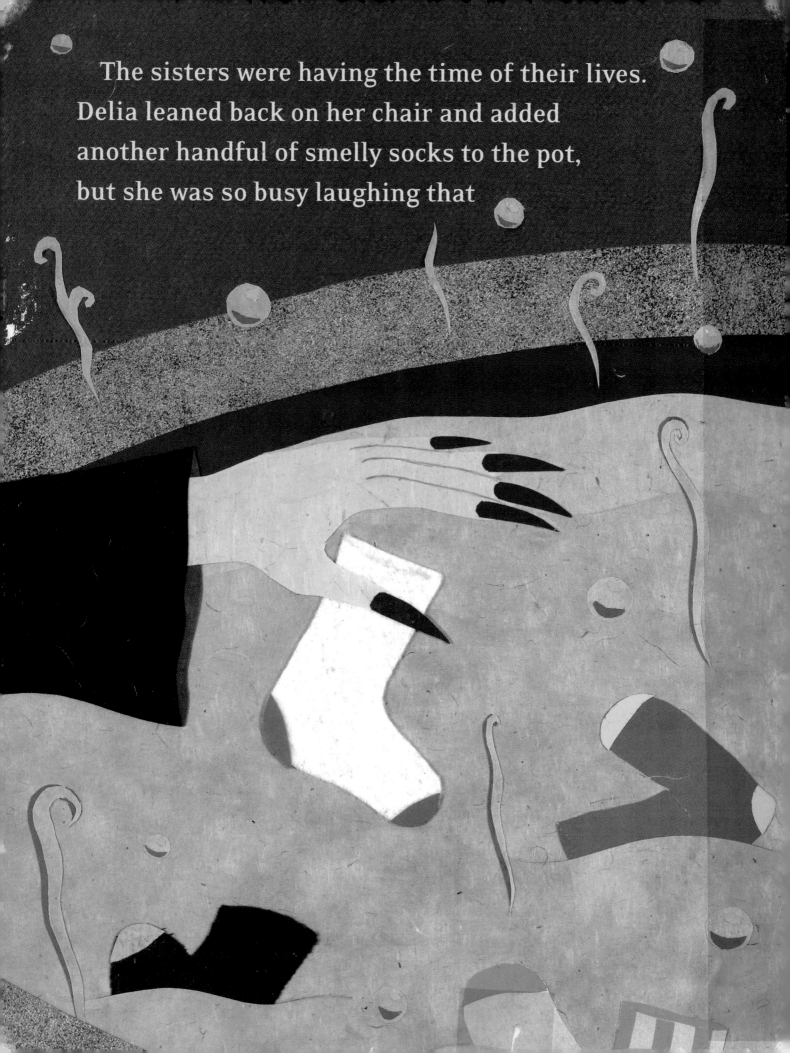

The sisters were having the time of their lives. Delia leaned back on her chair and added another handful of smelly socks to the pot, but she was so busy laughing that she didn't notice a clean baby's booty was mixed in with the stinky socks. Suddenly the nasty green smoke turned bright pink and was filling the house.

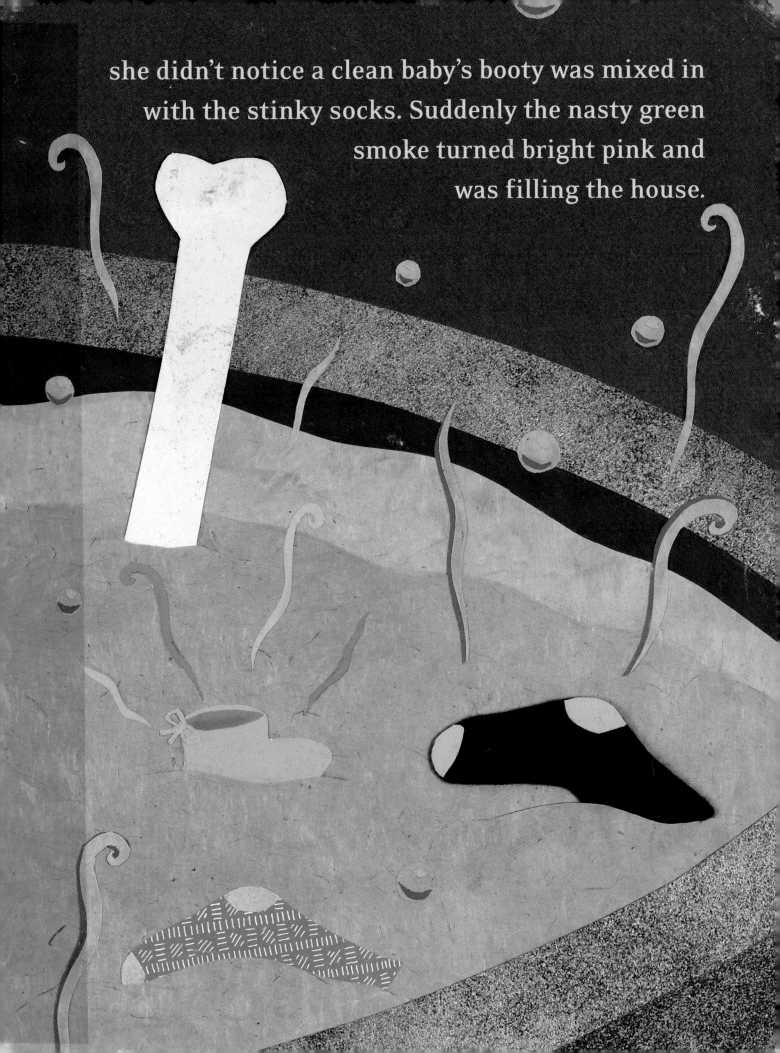

"OH, BATS!" screamed Ophelia. "What's gone wrong?"
Delia scooped out the baby booty, but it was too late.
More and more pretty pink smoke filled the house.
"Quick, dump the rest of those smelly socks into
the pot!" Ophelia yelled, but her voice was
getting softer and softer.

"What's happening to my voice?" she cooed.
Delia tried to talk, but what came out
was "Goo goo ga ga goo."

When the pink smoke finally cleared, the twins
had been turned into chubby little toddlers,
and they were very cute.
"Meeeoow," cried Rufus, who was now a little kitten.

Outside, the foul green smoke had faded,
and no more doors were slammed.
In fact, the children were extra polite,
so they got extra candy. The biggest
crowd was next door to the witches'
house. An old woman was giving out
fresh-baked chocolate-chip cookies
to the trick-or-treaters.

The next morning, the old woman
heard strange noises next door
and went over to see what was going on.
"Oh, how cute the two of you are," she said to the
tiny witch twins, even though they were scowling.
The woman brought them home with her and
put them in snuggly pink pajamas.

But as soon as their black dresses were off,
those girls started bawling, and nothing
could get them to stop.

So the sweet old woman sewed
a little black blanket for each of
the gloomy girls, and when they
weren't looking, she tied a pink bow
around their pointy black hats.

Rufus loved his new home.

Now, the neighborhood kids come over every day
after school. They eat cookies and milk and
try to get little Delia and Ophelia to smile.
Who knows?
Maybe they'll grow up a little nicer this time.

Lindsay Mayes

Chip Straniero

Lindsay Behnke

Attitude!

Jessica Helmstetter

Reilly's
sock
Do not clean!

Reilly Sheffield

Michael Yaccarino